# HORRiD HENRY'S
## Haunted House

# HORRiD HENRY'S
# Haunted House

Francesca Simon
*Illustrated by* Tony Ross

Orion
Children's Books

*Horrid Henry's Haunted House* originally appeared in
*Horrid Henry's Haunted House* first published in
Great Britain in 1999 by Orion Children's Books
This edition first published in Great Britain in 2014
by Orion Children's Books
a division of the Orion Publishing Group Ltd
Orion House
5 Upper Saint Martin's Lane
London WC2H 9EA
An Hachette UK Company

1 3 5 7 9 10 8 6 4 2

A catalogue record for this book is available from the British Library.

ISBN 978 1 4440 0907 1
Printed in China

www.orionbooks.co.uk
www.horridhenry.co.uk

# Contents

# Chapter 1

"No way!" shrieked Horrid Henry.
He was not staying the weekend with
his slimy cousin Stuck-Up Steve,
and that was that.

He sat in the back seat of the car
with his arms folded.

"Yes you are," said Mum.

"Steve can't wait to see you,"
said Dad.

This was not exactly true.
After Henry has sprayed Steve with
green goo last Christmas, *and* helped
himself to a few of Steve's presents,
Steve had sworn revenge.

Under the circumstances,
Henry thought it would be a good
idea to keep out of Steve's way.

And now Mum had arranged for him
to spend the weekend while she and
Dad went off on their own! Perfect
Peter was staying with Tidy Ted

and he was stuck
with Steve.

"It's a great chance for you boys to become good friends," Mum said. "Steve is a very nice boy."

# Chapter 2

"I feel sick," said Henry, coughing.

"Stop faking," said Mum.
"You were well enough to play
football all morning."

"I'm too tired," said Henry, yawning.

"I'm sure you'll get plenty of rest at Aunt Ruby's," said Dad firmly.

# "I'm not going!"

howled Henry.

Mum and Dad took Henry by the arms, dragged him to Rich Aunt Ruby's door, and rang the bell. The massive door opened immediately.

"Welcome, Henry,"
said Rich Aunt Ruby, giving him
a great smacking kiss.

"Henry, how lovely to see you,"
said Stuck-Up Steve sweetly.
"That's a very nice second-hand
jumper you're wearing."

"Hush, Steve," said Rich Aunt Ruby.
"I think Henry looks very smart."

Henry glared at Steve.
Thank goodness he'd remembered his
Goo-Shooter. He had a feeling
he might need it.

# Chapter 3

"Goodbye, Henry," said Mum. "Be good. Ruby, thank you so much for having him."

"Our pleasure," lied Aunt Ruby.

The great door closed.
Henry was alone in the house
with his arch-enemy.
Henry looked grimly at Steve.
What a horrible boy, he thought.
Steve looked grimly at Henry.
What a horrible boy, he thought.

"Why don't you both go upstairs and play in Steve's room till supper's ready?" said Aunt Ruby.

"I'll show Henry where he's sleeping first," said Steve.

"Good idea," said Aunt Ruby.

Reluctantly, Henry followed his cousin up the wide staircase.

"I bet you're scared of the dark," said Steve.

"'Course I'm not," said Henry.

"That's good," said Steve. "This is my room," he added, opening the door to an enormous bedroom. Horrid Henry stared longingly at the shelves filled to bursting with zillions of toys and games.

"Of course all *my* toys are brand new. Don't you dare touch anything," hissed Steve. "They're all mine and only *I* can play with them."

Henry scowled.
When he was king he'd use Steve's
head for target practice.

They continued all the way to
the top. Goodness, this old house
was big, thought Henry.

Steve opened the door to a
large attic bedroom, with brand new
pink and blue flowered wallpaper,
a four-poster bed, an enormous
polished wood wardrobe, and
two large windows.

"You're in the haunted room,"
said Steve casually.

"Great!" said Henry. "I love ghosts."
It would take more than a silly ghost
to frighten *him*.

"Don't believe me if you don't want to," said Steve. "Just don't blame me when the ghost starts wailing."

"You're nothing but a big fat liar," said Henry.

He was **sure**
Steve was
lying.

He was
**absolutely
sure**
Steve was lying.

He was **one million
percent sure**
that Steve was lying.

He's just trying to pay me back for
Christmas, thought Henry.
Steve shrugged. "Suit yourself.
See that stain on the carpet?"
Henry looked down at something
brownish.

"That's where the ghost vaporized," whispered Steve. "Of course if you're too scared to sleep here..."

Henry would rather have walked on hot coals than admit being scared to Steve.

He yawned, as if he'd never heard
anything so boring.
"I'm looking forward to meeting
the ghost," said Henry.

"Good," said Steve.

"Supper, boys!" called Aunt Ruby.

# Chapter 4

Henry lay in bed.

Somehow he'd survived the dreadful meal and Stuck-Up Steve's bragging about his expensive clothes, toys and trainers.

Now here he was, alone in the attic at the top of the house. He'd jumped into bed, carefully avoiding the faded brown patch on the floor.
He was sure it was just spilled cola or something, but just in case...

Henry looked around him.
The only thing he didn't like was
the huge wardrobe opposite the bed.

It loomed up in the darkness
at him. You could hide a body
in that wardrobe, thought Henry,
then rather wished he hadn't.

# "Ooooooooooh."

Henry stiffened. Had he just imagined the sound of someone moaning?

## Silence.

Nothing, thought Henry, snuggling down under the covers. Just the wind.

"Oooooooooh."

This time the moaning was a
fraction louder. The hairs on
Henry's neck stood up.
He gripped the sheets tightly.

"Haaaaaahhhhhhhh."

Henry sat up.

"Haaaaaahhhhhhhh."

The ghostly breathy moaning sound
was not coming from outside.
It appeared to be coming from
inside the giant wardrobe.
Quickly, Henry switched on
the bedroom light.

What am I going to do?
thought Henry. He wanted to
run screaming to his aunt.
But the truth was, Henry was
too frightened to move.

Some dreadful moaning thing
was inside the wardrobe.
Just waiting to get *him*.

And then Horrid Henry
remembered who he was.
Leader of a pirate gang.
Afraid of nothing (except injections).

I'll just get up and check inside
that wardrobe, he thought.
Am I a man or a mouse?
Mouse! he thought.

# Chapter 5

He did not move.

# "Ooooooaaaahhhh,"

moaned the **thing**.
The unearthly noises were
getting louder.

Shall I wait for **it** to get me,
or shall I make a move first?
thought Henry. Silently,
he reached under the bed for
his Goo-Shooter.

Then slowly, he swung his feet
over the bed.

Tiptoe.
Tiptoe.
Tiptoe.

Holding his breath, Horrid Henry
stood outside the wardrobe.

"HAHAHAHAHAHAHAHAHHA!"

Henry jumped. Then he flung open
the door and fired.

Splat!

# "AHAHAHAHA HAHAHAHAHA ughhhhhhh—"

The wardrobe was empty.

Except for something small and
greeny-black on the top shelf.
It looked like – it was!

Henry reached up and took it.
It was a CD player.
Covered in green goo.
Inside was a CD. It was called
"Dr Jekyll's Spooky Sounds."

Steve, thought Horrid Henry grimly.

# Revenge!

# Chapter 6

"Did you sleep well, dear?"
asked Aunt Ruby at breakfast.

"Like a log," said Henry.

"No strange noises?" asked Steve.

"No," smiled Henry sweetly.
"Why, did you hear something?"

Steve looked disappointed.
Horrid Henry kept his face blank.
He couldn't wait for the evening.

Horrid Henry spent a busy day.
He went ice-skating.

He went to the cinema.

He played football.

After supper, Henry went
straight to bed.
"It's been a lovely day," he said.
"But I'm tired. Goodnight,
Aunt Ruby. Goodnight, Steve."

"Goodnight, Henry," said Ruby.
Steve ignored him.

But Henry did not go to
his bedroom. Instead he sneaked
into Steve's. He wriggled under
Steve's bed and lay there, waiting.

# Chapter 7

Soon Steve came into the room. Henry resisted the urge to reach out and seize Steve's skinny leg. He had something much scarier in mind.

He heard Steve putting on his blue bunny pyjamas and jumping into bed.

Henry waited until the room was dark.

Steve lay above him, humming to himself.
"Dooby dooby dooby do," sang Steve.

Slowly, Henry reached up, and ever so slightly, poked the mattress.

# Silence.

"Dooby dooby dooby do," sang Steve, a little more quietly.

Henry reached up and poked the mattress again.

Steve sat up. Then he lay back.

Henry poked the mattress again,
ever so slightly.

"Must be my imagination,"
muttered Steve.

Henry allowed several moments to
pass. Then he twitched the duvet.

"Mummy," whimpered Steve.

Jab! Henry gave the mattress
a definite poke.

## "Ahhhhhhhhhhhh!"
screamed Steve. He leaped up
and ran out of the room.

## "Mummy! Help!
Monsters!"

Henry scrambled out of the room
and ran silently up to his attic.
Quick as he could he put on his
pyjamas, then clattered noisily back
down the stairs to Steve's.

Aunt Ruby was on her hands and
knees, peering under the bed.
Steve was shivering and quivering
in the corner.

"There's nothing here, Steve,"
she said firmly.

"What's wrong?" asked Henry.

"Nothing," muttered Steve.

"You're not *scared* of the dark, are you?" said Henry.

"Back to bed, boys," said Aunt Ruby. She left the room.

"Ahhhhh, Mummy, help! Monsters!" mimicked Henry, sticking out his tongue.

"Mum!" wailed Steve.
"Henry's being horrid!"

# "Go to bed, both of you!"
shrieked Ruby.

"Watch out for monsters," said Henry.
Steve did not move from his corner.

"Want to swap rooms tonight?"
said Henry.

Steve did not wait to be asked twice.
"Oh yes," said Steve.

"Go on up," said Henry.
"Sweet dreams."

Steve dashed out of his bedroom as
fast as he could.

Tee hee, thought Horrid Henry, pulling Steve's toys down from the shelves. Now, what would he play with first?

Oh, yes. He'd left a few spooky sounds of his own under the attic bed – just in case.